Y0-AGU-007

OTHER FUGITIVES

AND

OTHER STRANGERS

OTHER FUGITIVES
AND
OTHER STRANGERS

RIGOBERTO GONZÁLEZ

TUPELO PRESS

For Eric-Christopher

Other Fugitives and Other Strangers
© Copyright 2006 Rigoberto González

ISBN 10: 1-932195-49-1
ISBN 13: 978-1-932195-49-1
Printed in Canada

All rights reserved.
No part of this book may be reproduced
without the permission of the publisher.

First paperback edition November 2006
Library of Congress Control Number: 2006901778

Tupelo Press
Post Office Box 539, Dorset, Vermont 05251
(802) 366-8185
(802) 362-1883 fax
www.tupelopress.org

Cover and book design by Josef Beery
Cover painting, *Wrestlers*, by Thomas Eakins

Supported in part by an award from
the National Endowment for the Arts

NATIONAL
ENDOWMENT
FOR THE ARTS

Muchísimas gracias

to all my friends—too many to name here—who
offered meals, conversations and spare beds (or
couches) during the critical periods in the life of
this book. I must however, single out Bino and
the Realuyo family—maraming salamat po. Many
thanks to Eduardo C. Corral for helping me give
order to this chaotic project. Gracias Gary Soto.
Abrazos fuertes, Lauro Flores y Christine Yuodelis-
Flores. And as always, much love and appreciation
to Minnie Bruce Pratt, Pat Mora, Maurya Simon,
Denise Duhamel and Scott Hightower for the many
words of wisdom and encouragement. Also, it is
with much gratitude that I acknowledge the John
Simon Guggenheim Memorial Foundation and la
Fundación Valparaíso of Mojácar, Spain for the
generous support.

Acknowledgments

5 AM
"Good Boy"
"Sweet Somnambulist"

AMERICAS REVIEW
"From the Wake of a Former Lover"
"Of Despots and Deities"
"The Untimely Return of My Dead"

EL ANDAR
"Neurotic Double"

CHELSEA
"Changng Your New Year's Tune"
"My Crush on the Crisis Counselor"

CHURCH-WELLESLEY REVIEW
(online)
"Latin Lover"
"Breaking Down Picasso's Minotaur"

CLACKAMAS LITERARY REVIEW
"Crooked Man"

COLORADO REVIEW
"Papi Love"
"Other Fugitives and Other Strangers"

FISHOUSE (online)
"Danza Macabre"

FLYWAY
"Skins Preserve Us"
"La Pelona at Her Dressing Table"
"Sleeping with the Politician"
"Vanquishing Act"

HEArt
"Rapist: A Romance"

THE IOWA REVIEW
"Transference"

ISLE REVIEW (online)
"In Praise of the Mouth"
"Trace"

LODESTAR QUARTERLY (online)
"Other Victims"
"Widower's Welcome"

MODERN WORDS
"The Balloon Artist"

LA PETITE ZINE (online)
"The Man Who Left You"
"Point It Out"
"Breads That Hunger"

NOTRE DAME REVIEW
"Dear Dead Lover"

PRAIRIE SCHOONER
"Scar"

SOLO
"Freak"

ZYZZYVA
"Welts off the Bone"

"Rapist: A Romance" appears in *Like Thunder: Poets Respond to Violence in America*, ed. Virgil Suárez and Ray G. Van Cleave (Iowa City: University of Iowa Press, 2002).

This book of poems was a finalist for the Alice Fay Di Castagnola Award from the Poetry Society of America.

Contents

PART III

~ ~ ~

PART I

~ ~ ~

Body, remember not only how much you were loved

Cavafy

Good Boy

Wasn't I a good boy once? Wasn't I
once stripped of body hair and knuckle, a laugh
so clean it stretched like a white sheet on the clothesline?
Wasn't my voice once
the contagious note of a two-finger bell?

The rust in my throat now coats those high-pitch sounds.
If there is a child in me, he hides
behind the dull flint of my hip. Not alive,
not dead, but lost in the stomach
to dissolve like any other

color. Old photographs don't persuade me
that I could have grown into a man
who could love other men with self-restraint,
who would not ask a man to sleep
on the sharp blades of the bed

without complaints. Surely my anger had
always been squatting on its claws, eager
to tear its way out of my ten-year-old ribs.
Then how do you explain this
strange ability to inflict pain?

I must have ingested hatred
through the spoons of my childhood.
I must have been the changeling matured

now longing for things that blister
and boil. Whatever you place in my hand

I want to puncture out
of mischief. Or perhaps the intentional act
of uncoiling comfort is to get
at its irritated heart and confirm that
even the purest odor stings.

Lover, when I drive the nails to your chest
your mouth opens, white
and pasty like a moon. Do you
see me waving back twenty years ago
from the distant planets of my eyes?

Scar

How deep is your love? How
deep does the razor sink
into your cheek before
you taste it? Only trees

know the blade's invasion,
the evidence engraved.
But no oak's battle scar
will be immortalized

so fiercely. You love me!
The exclamation mark
will hide beneath your skin
but it will scream and scream

like the whistles of those
distant streets you wander,
where your stitches flaunt
to strangers the ghostly sheen

of a clean incision—
so exact, a master-
piece. The craftsmanship's mine;
that is my signature.

A vision called to me:
on your face the beauty

of a knife slit haunted
me, so I carved it free.

I hold your head up like
a trophy, rub your scar.
Please promise it won't cut
back. I don't like to bleed.

The Balloon Artist

With each kiss he sucks more air out of his lover's mouth.
When he reaches down to pinch flesh, he expects
an elastic resistance, but instead gets
flesh, disappointingly soft and passive—
no snap to it at all. It's an imperfect surface:

lumps, calluses, sores, inconsistent in dimension
and texture. Even the temperatures vary: the neck rises to warmth,
the valley of the back falls to chilly; the belly remains
an undecided horizon, gathering heat and cooling off
each time their bodies come together, then separate.

How he longs for the resilience of a skin
that will reject a tactile history, that is
unsentimental about prodding and contusions.
Balloons are ideal in that way: they can be stretched,
squeezed and twisted into quiet complacency.

Unlike weary lovers, balloons vanish with one quick
burst when they deplete their use, or they sneak
out subtly, shrinking back into the zeroes of the universe.
Few hang on like the body here beneath him that denies its own
deflation, its nightly flattening into exhausted rubber.

Point It Out

Your finger is a barb on a hook is a prong.
Resting on my arm it is not as dangerous
as when it sinks into my mouth. Inside me
it's as cool as a thermometer making room, inciting
longings for a toxic taste.

If I'm careless I'll spill the tongue's blood.
It would like that, that finger, having offered me
every other part of my body
on those nights when nights bump elbows when
the crescent moon is just another sharp threat.

My kind believes that a splinter in the fingertip
will travel through the vein and stop
the heart once it plunges in. I suspect
you slip your finger in me while I sleep,
expecting me to suck the menace out.

The Man Who Left You

did not come back. He sent another man
not a man, but a five-fingered web
that muzzles your heart shut at night.
The man who left you was more than that—
five-fingered, yes, but a fist

sometimes gentle as a rose—
knuckles tender-petaled into sleep. You wished
to cut it off at the twisted root, replant it,
let another man grow out of it,
exchange the shards of your insomnia for a bed.

But the man who's here instead has
a familiar hand, bones thick with threats.
It hasn't struck you yet, but it will,
like the hand of the man who left you.
At least that hand stood still when still.

Other Victims

Thank heavens for victims who find their way
to folly. They walk on the lean streets in your place
and into a world rich with abuses. Their fates would have
no place to shine if not for that journey, the possible
headlines, and sigh pushed out by the odd relief that

it wasn't you. You are lucky. The man you live with
would never kill you, not in the violent way
other people die, all horror-flick theatrics with costumes
so dirty they could only thrive in other parts of town,
not here in the quiet rooms where your only surprise

is a kiss from behind. If he ever wanted to be rid of you,
your lover would do it kindly: perhaps a poison that falls in love
with your sleep. A compassionate man, he won't let you die
in public, or alone. He won't let you suffer
without him. Never worry. He'll take care of you at home.

Crooked Man

He owns a crooked tongue
that jams his grief inside his crooked mouth
and no one hears the news that
I have died.

Neighbors say I'm still inside
his crooked house, which, when I entered
months ago was not a dark cocoon of wood
and bone. I should have known

better, people will declare when
I'm finally extracted like a nail.
But until then I'm not mistaken in
the kinder things I've learned

about this man who wants to change his crooked, crooked
ways. He apologizes when he strikes, he
craves forgiveness. When I drop it
on his tongue he savors it—

coaxes out the peppermint
to soothe my wounds. No touch
can heal the way his does, starving pain away
with promises. No promises can hold more hollow bowls.

Only Bluebeard's wives have grown
so wise, seeking out forbidden rooms

because they want to wear the secret of their lover's
lust—passion so dangerous it's fatal.

This man I love will never tell
his side of it. He mourns in silence.
If only he could sing my ecstasy—imprisonment
within his crooked, crooked heart.

Of Despots and Deities

"Who'll ever witness the end of this pot?"
Abuelo said, and I didn't have the courage to tell him
he was pointing out the griddle—a coarse pupil, cloudy
as his. Had he tried to lift it, his wrist would have
snapped, and then the discharge of old hornets from the marrow.

> *The finger-painted spots of your nipples*
> *have always known. You see their reflections*
> *in everything round; they inhabit the kitchens*
> *of your adolescence. When your pupils widen*
> *you love your nude body all over again.*

Anger tapers off, but its sick flame only sickens.
I watch him trim the hairs in his ear, his hand steady
with the scissors, that cruel advisor. All things feminine
get cut: pink ribbons, knitting yarn, and little girls who play
hopscotch inside little boys. At night the cries of dolls melting.

> *The wooden stirrings in your mouth*
> *have always known. Whisper, and the splinters*
> *betray your secret lust for cut-out clothing.*
> *Paper dresses and orange skirts with white paper*
> *hinges unsettle the mothballs in your stomach.*

Beatings shape the man over manhood's anvil. Abuelo
taught me to spit with blood and to curse with the deep voice

I'd later seek from other men. The bully who kicks me
comes back to massage my injury. The purple cross
of his foot was just another form of brutal love.

The red kisses of your wrists have always
known. Men will want to trap you in-
side the butterfly jars of their fists. Beware
of air-holes that look like stars.
Even grandfathers can play false gods.

I unmourn the murdered sissy of my youth,
the sack of discarded pigtails and puckered lips that
burst like an appendix. I hold my scar for the man
who'll split it open with his gorgeous thumbs, who with his
teeth will liberate the pin-pierced mariposa of my tongue.

Sweet Somnambulist

Lights off
and your weight drifts on top of me again.
I pretend you're stirring in your own
bed in case your father wakes.
No bedroom doors. Curtains.
The squeaky bed startles me repeatedly
since the house dilates with darkness
and every room empties into this one.
Your father snores across the hallway
but when the curtain shifts I think I see him
peering in, bewildered by the bulk beneath the covers,
the rhythmic flow of shadows, the moans—warm
scent of our mouths—that belong inside some other
room, some other night when your mother was alive
and naked as a bowl of berries.
Our sounds excite his sleep: I hear him
murmuring. Your mother's name? Mine?
When you bite into my neck, I reach back
and touch your father's face, warn him
to be careful. He pushes deeper into me, my flesh
swallows his body hair, the black coffee of his tongue.
It is you, my silent lover, I lose in the dark
and not the widower who offered me a home
as if I were his second son.
At breakfast, he will smile across the table,

he will clear his throat with the grunt I've had all night

to memorize, and I'll be here again,

flung onto the mattress with him.

My Crush on the Crisis Counselor

How is it, good doctor,

that your eye won't dry up,

soaking up dawn after dawn

of would-be suicides?

The pupil floats as rigid

as a lily pad over that

polluted iris, crystallized

into bulletproof glass.

Has it been cauterized—

a rubber stump built to bounce off

threats of scissors, knives?

Still it looks scratched—

an old record stuck to its

needle-addict groove. The blues

fade in and out, staggering

with motion sickness.

I'm impressed by its ability

to hold down what it swallows: a crooked

horizon of eyelids on a thirst-

twisted drama queen sleepy as a moth.

Your eyes belly out, good doctor,

fragile as soap bubbles,

yet they absorb razors point blank
without blowing up. At night

does your lover
empty them out like wastebaskets?
Does he scrape off
stubborn patients like hardened rice?

Would it surprise you
to go blind, having run
out of your vision like the ink
of your fountain pen,

having drained it, drop
by drop of its blood?
I still have mine,
the drop you placed on my palm—

a lozenge the size
of an antidepressant tablet,
inedible yet voracious
as a dead star.

Sometimes it sticks to the door
like a keyhole, sucking in
an entire room in one sitting.
Sometimes it burrows a glory-

hole in the toilet room, small

enough to fit a single cock.
But the damn thing is
always hungry,

shrinking shrinking
as it consumes its own rind.
Once it is gone,
I'll have nothing, no one.

That's why I'm here
again, good doctor, couch-thick
inside this shirt, taut as girdle and
unfashionable as plain white sheets.

I've come for another dose
of advice, for that watery look, cute
as a centerfold's, that distills my bad
dreams with a flash of light.

Neurotic Double

I'm not ashamed of my naked body,
my naked body is ashamed of me,
of how I tinge
and stain him, then blame him for what I did.
We sleep together
but it's me up nights, scratching at his ankle
till he bleeds, till he turns and tips his mouth
like a black-lipped mug airing dry its crusts.
He's all crusts—ear, anus, eyelid's grin—
and our armpits scrape the other's shoulders clean
and the noise keeps the orange trees awake.
When I touch him I'm wiping off my hands,
losing a finger each night on the edges of his skin,
then growing that finger back the next morning
because mourning is generous.
But there are always traces of spills and clots
sunk deep as navels on the mattress, red
as the only red that can escape the touch
of the tongue's comfort-seeking tip.
But not having that tongue print, claims my body,
worries him.

In Praise of the Mouth

Your throat, moan-cluttered, opens
like the desert's flower. The tongue quivering with thirst
is not the stamen, but the wet union of exposed
corolla and nocturnal bat—the sharp sting
of pink, the accidental fang of red. With me inside,
your mouth transforms into a pair of leeches
fattening sucker to sucker, an
uroboros swallowing its glutinous reflection
to retrieve a slick coat as it spits itself back.
Neck against neck, two voices dance
through the madness of the Venus's-fly-trap, the rattle
in the hinges of its blade is not
death, but the cry of love—what the narcissistic
moon hums to the sea that mirrors it.
Even the alligator's dangerous parade of teeth
looks beautiful because it celebrates the mouth.
With or without the ringing uvula of welcomes
your cave still softens into silk
when something finds its refuge there. And there
stone shatters, undressed of blue crystals,
bone melts to marrow, and hearts implode,
shriveling down to the plum pit origins of lust.

Dear Dead Lover

Had I turned to stone before you shot me
the bullet would have
bounced off my cheek and I would've sported
a beauty mark for all eternity. Mine
the vanity of Michelangelo's David. But I didn't

and now I wonder if my injury
lacking pattern or creative intuition
becomes me. Does red flatter my complexion?
Does the milky flesh of shock?
Am I staring left or right? Talk to me

about my eyes, how they escaped
my skull like the cherries on a slot machine.
Talk to me about my mouth and how enamel
changes color with the sudden rage
of gunfire. Tell me that my smile

remains intact. The only mirrors here
my hands and death
like an exhausted hound sleeps over
them. Lover, oh predictably impulsive lover,
through your pang of guilt tell me

how prettier I look dead, no longer aging or
battling the diet pills, thirty-three years old forever,

permanently size thirty-four. I'm all ears again.
Well, maybe only one, but blame
your drunken aim for that. In any case,

I'm listening. I hear you moaning
the woe of silent movie screens in
empty theaters not yet swept. Your soul lies
flat like the solitary broom. Forgive my
ill-timed poetry, but romantic thoughts console me—

I'm frightened by the literal tongue
of silence. Keep talking, lover,
tell me more about my eyes, how stunning
my white carnations, how arresting
their gloss. If I could cry I'd leave

petals at your feet. But I can't
so in the place of tears take
the blood drops with you. Collect them
off the wall, the floor, my skin, before
they crawl away like ladybugs. Tell me

the clear jellyfish of your heart
reddens once again because I set it
pulsing with my pardon. Tell me
that you'll miss me. Here. I'm giving you
the words. Now say it. Say it once more.

PART II

~ ~ ~

ay, cuerpo mío, tan huerfano de amor,
cómo me duele haberte negado tanto,
ahora quisiera besarte hasta el hueso

Francisco X. Alarcón

Skins Preserve Us

Pick another body. Any
body. All bodies recognize
similar functions.

If you move
it learns
to move with you:

its foot imitates
your foot; its nipples stiffen
to mimic yours;

the thumb, that absent-
minded wanderer, eventually
matches your thumb.

Pick a body: limb
by limb, bone
by bone—one tooth

at a time,
screwing each molar,
each incisor,

into your own white gums.
Don't be hasty
selecting a tongue—

sample enough of them
to make a wise decision.
Sample plenty since

tongues tend to be
fastidious, unlike
the gullible anus or seductive

cock, both easy
to please. Fat hearts
adapt as quickly as elbows

and knees. Everything is
interchangeable. Entire
bodies, replaceable.

Including yours.
The body you wear now became
sick from overuse.

Your lover
simply left, leaving you
temporarily untouchable

with a body
thick with bruises,
thin-skinned to near-

transparency.
Before you disappear
completely, pick another

body, another mouth,
another pair of hands, softer
than the ones that used to

touch you. Pick at
another face, but careful
with the eyes.

Snap each one
into your hollow
sockets, make sure

they'll hold
down the lonely
dawns with you.

La Pelona at Her Dressing Table

She screws the eyeballs on like bulbs,
both locked to a hatpin's blade
for sharper vision. She

resets the teeth—now straight
as a pew of church girls. Her bite,
shoe-tap clear with a slice

of pink skin zippered on
the jaw to complete the mouth.
Two smaller pieces flap

over each eye, the fringed muscles color-
matched to the earlobes dangling from
porcelain hooks. She

flicks one ear to make it ring, but only
the dull memory of her lover's
nibble echoes in the hollow

of the ducts. She slips a mask
over her bald head, tightens it
at the center of the face, and

calls the knot a nose. She stretches
the body glove taut, but nippled
at the ends of fingers,

toes. The chest balloons as she
inflates the heart, lungs,
belly, breasts. Her penis

limp as a rooster comb
she tucks against the perineum,
neatly as a bookmark.

For a tongue, she guts
a glamour magazine, shoves the covers
between her squeaky cheeks.

Head cocked, she
snags a black wig. Dissatisfied she
throws it back to the dresser.

The hair drops open
like the wings of a dead crow. She
grins at her sudden

art, at the mirror's willingness
for illusion. Down here, a stiff
bird on polished wood. Up

there, an impeccable coiffure,
groomed and glittered into
feminine spectacle—

the woman she knows
she was. The woman she can't
reject. That woman.

Sleeping with the Politician

Even the lights are a negotiation:
off? or on?
Tonight he wants to see himself

exchange a mouth for a kiss.
But he takes much more than that,
tearing off any other kiss I might have

bargained with. They peel away like rind.
My shadow jitters, then stiffens
like a stain against the wall.

My lover feeds and fattens.
Still I apologize for my face, empty
as a pocket. The tongue leather-

numb. But this keen scavenger
finds value in that vacancy and stuffs it
with himself—cock, finger, foot.

He smiles at the window,
the window grins back, gulping down
the shrill of stars. The fist-tight

moon quivers
in its slow asphyxiation.
My hand seeks my lover's touch

but that touch too has a cost—
a sigh, bed-flat, a hollow moan,
my hand's dead weight.

I settle for an accidental brushing
of our wrists and call that
chemistry. I accept his

muscle spasms—the flesh
jutting toward my body
heat—and declare it love.

But there's a justice to all
this give and take, an exchange
not even he suspects

each time our bodies meet.
For every joint or tough appendage
my lover claims as his

I repossess, word by word,
my fevered mutterings. Slowly
I unstick each promise,

diminishing
the odds against my favor.
Tomorrow he'll forget

to take my kisses with him
and I'll eat them
like a cup of figs.

Next Saturday he won't remember
where I leave the extra key
and it will breathe in peace

for an entire week.
But my greatest victory: when
in a month he can't recall

my name, the purple weight of
my favorite sheets; when in a year
he wonders where that sullen pout

he carries came from,
and for whose sorrow on the forehead
did he trade in his own.

Vanquishing Act

Disrupting symmetry: the key
to the art of conquering

a lover. Take exactitude and
distort its vain

proportions. Cover the navel: de-
center the belly; hide

one nipple: lose half
the torso; conceal

the sex beneath the cold
knuckle: disorient the groin. Fitting

substitute: mouth.
Swallow ear, chin, nose. Tug

appendages like Picasso's
canvas. Like a wet brush

stroke them flat. Say
minus. Say cancellation.

Negate one leg,
wedge your foot between

the ankles, divide
knees. Lock the limbs into a

landscape of
irregularity. Splinter shadow,

dent bone.
Variation: plunge the face,

tongue—that
practiced breacher—

into the river of thighs.
Claim all other estuaries:

tear elbow from
rib, split buttocks, dig deep

into the root of armpits,
anus, throat—

thrust them inside
out. Bandage the missing skin

with yours. Fill up the craters
in the flesh. Graft hair.

Make him so much you

only you can make him.

Complete dominion:
unlock the shoulders,

snap the clavicle,
collapse the spine.

The pelvic bone folds
inward, the foreskin back.

Femur slips inside tibia
like a pipe. Press down

firmly. Muscle pleats.
Say fraction, say rhomboid

suitcase—magician's box
that opens at the jaw.

Inside, the heart keeps pumping
like an anxious rabbit.

Rushing to the Cemetery

1. The Trespass

Dismissed, matching buttons.
Unfurled, similar cloaking sheets. The belt hinge
snaps twice, losing its patience
to the hunger of zippers unlocking their teeth.

It has been that long, caretaker, that brief—
those fingerings across a skin with hair.
You envy them, these men who jumped the wall
to wipe the dust off a grave.

One man polishes the tile until it squeaks, the other
groans, startling the owl off its perch.
A white feather slides down the speckled sky.
You follow it, you crouch into the dewy grass with it,

you comfort it against your cheek
from the tremors in the ground—
the sounds of bones gnawing
anxiously through silk, omnivorous as shrews.

2. Night Vision

When the car strikes the cemetery wall head-on
it doesn't go completely through
the way the driver's

skull penetrates the web
of windshield, shedding the face—
pushing out a smile, no teeth.

Strands of blood caress
the vehicle's bent curve.
The hot hood pops

up to cool the pipes;
the engine's breath is spent
at the force of the midnight

meeting. The man's hand swollen
as a boxing glove stuffs itself
into the dash. A stone chip dives

down to greet the knuckle
pressed crack against crack to the glass.
And the back seat finally doubles

over with exhaustion,
silencing the memory of its passion-
heavy indentations—the tongue-to-tongue

scuffles lost that pushed the driver's
foot into the pedal.
The letter in his pocket dampens

to illegibility. The letter in the mail
falls flat under the rubber heel
of a RETURN TO SENDER stamp.

The door swings open. Out
drops the solitary shoe
with its stunned, empty mouth.

3. *Moribund*

Lover, what beautiful toes you have.
Even if it's dead

this practice of finding solace
in rubbing the feet against the top

of another Catholic's head, I've enjoyed
that digging of my scalp with

your tiny muscles softening, warm
in a coat of camphor oil.

Tomorrow you'll lie flat on a bier, your feet
balanced on the heels,

but I'll remember your feet like this:
a pair of wet tongues,

pink and sensitive
like the valley of your groin.

I touch the grooves and feel you
shudder—stay ticklish to the end.

Wrap my hands around your ankles,
attach your tendons to my bones,

and take me with you.
I fit you like a coffin—

your body slipping back into itself.

Freak

She was born a he,

a mass of heavy dark muscle that forced his father

to drink. No sober evening met

that peephole of an eye that held

its breath when nurse or visitor looked in.

The baby's limbs were pasted

to the torso, the fingers, tightly stitched, unlike

the penis, which curved and curved

into a soft solitary wrinkle.

To watch his son suckle was to witness

his wife's breast turn itself inside out.

From this creature, feared the father,

a monster: chain and leash, circus

freakdom, a parade of pink dwarves, bearded

women, and a four-legged body with two somber skulls.

Worse yet, a salivating canine of a boy

squatting in triumph over the rubbery flesh

of its mother. But for all ill-fated scenarios

the father could conceive, nothing

prepared him for the sultry

woman his son became.

The boy bloomed inside seductive

lavenders. Greens plump as pears gave him hips;

sunflower yellows and magentas warmly breathing
taught him how to wiggle and

whisper. At night the mysteries of red
revealed themselves to him—to her.
The father trembled at the passion stirred
within him. All those years
of resisting touch and kiss had swollen up into

temptation at the sight of her—
his son reversed into the beauty of
pleated skirts, lace ribbons, nylons
opaque as smoky bars.
Unable to escape desire

the father grasped a shattered bottle
then plunged himself
into this creature's bed, tearing
cloth from skin, hair from scalp,
flesh from bones—the lady's lovely bones.

The Untimely Return of My Dead

With three loud knocks my dead lover
makes himself known. His first complaints, I suspect:
Why did you change the locks? Why, goddamit,
did you bury me in blue? Makes me look fat, for crissake!

But just as he surprised me with his death,
the dark flower of his hand blooming with the wonder
of its veins exposed—the face in every photograph
stunned by the shout of broken glass—

he surprised me with his untimely return.
More than frightened I feel cheated having
learned to appreciate my skin without
the imposition of his tongue or temper. My touch

now familiar with the act of
touch without reprimand. And lately
even my mouth has begun to overcome its shyness,
welcoming words like a strong flock of swallows

and not like the panic of bats. Three more knocks.
That these walls became my allies in favoring the modesty
of still-life over the conceit of my former lover's nudes
gave me courage to stay in the white

recliner. He gave up ownership when he died in it
and furniture is fickle: the bed

has forgotten its regular load, adjusted to my body
now divorced from the rigor of pretending rest.

The night sweats soaked into the mattress long
evaporated. Unlike my dead lover, I refuse to
choose the day I shock the world. There's no
mystery left in suicide. The challenge is, my love,

to keep yourself awake
despite the sleeping pill doses of sickness and
despair. What simple miracle you could have
learned had you used your ears on me and not

your hands. The knocking stops. I'm relieved
and saddened, that even in his death he cannot piece
himself together. And in the streets his wardrobe runs
away from him, divided among different men.

Rapist: A Romance

The quarter shined on his palm like light entering a hole in the bone. If fear had color his hand would have bruised. I wanted to place the tip of my nipple on the icy metal just to understand him a little more. Instead I took the coin and watched his body float backwards as if I had lifted its last anchor. He waved goodbye. The last speech in his mouth spilled out the way I had made him give up his words many times: thickly and slowly and red.

~ ~ ~

Our first night together I watched him sleep so peacefully I could have slit his throat. I held the tip of the knife inside his nostril, his ear, his navel; he might have itched in his dream. I let him live through the night and I knew he would leave me some day. The next morning I kissed his eyes through the lenses of his glasses. I disappeared behind the smudges. It was useless to see me coming.

~ ~ ~

I called him Pretty Cock because it was so perfect when it stiffened into carved stone. The skin of its head matched the nipples matched the anus and I realized what a simple confection he was. I confirmed it by what small imagination he displayed when he left and came back to me, wearing the same socks, speaking the same basic vocabulary of *love* and *yes* and *no* and *please*.

~ ~ ~

He was irresistible in that white terry cloth robe that curtained the hairy hamstrings of his legs as he bent over to check the bath. He was irresistible in the wet sleeve letting go of its clear coins on the black bathroom tile. He was irresistible slumped across the bathtub with the dark algae of his hair opening and closing on the surface of the water. Fucking him while he almost drowned—that was irresistible.

~ ~ ~

He told me how when he was twelve his mother had killed herself while he watched from the door as she took pill after pill as if in a trance. I told him how when I was fourteen my father had watched me do sit-ups in the living room until the night he pulled my legs over his shoulders and made me shit on his cock. He told me he had tried to kill himself the same way his mother had. I told him I didn't have a choice either.

~ ~ ~

Amor, I miss pressing my tongue to your pulse as I clench your wrist between my teeth. I miss the discovery of your heartbeat as I bite your neck. You said we fucked like cats and that night you clawed your way out from under me and made me chase you to the balcony. I pressed against you on the railing. I miss your back magnet-sticky on my chest like that. I could have pierced you perfectly so that your head slid painlessly through the moon's silver ring. But I missed.

~ ~ ~

I saw him waiting for the bus one afternoon. The black coat made him look like a piece of iron balanced on the curb.

I wanted to push it forward to flatten on the street with the heavy clang of metal vibrating through every vein of concrete. But I wasn't letting go that easily. Not yet. Not with that quarter still burning a hole in my stomach since the last time he left. He said to call him once I got over my fist-to-jaw reflex and I swallowed the coin just to spite him.

From the Wake of a Former Lover

You escaped the funeral,
fleeing from the man who can no longer walk,
who at one time borrowed your shoes.
Tonight he wore your black jacket

with those buttons that glared on his chest
like a row of stowaways. You
face the bathroom mirror—your skin
the same trap for stale light

as his. You take off your grieving
clothes, watch yourself naked against the wall—
your shadow dimming and dividing
like that upraised coffin's lid. All curves,

all upturned cups, your shadow draws an outline
of diluted color about to fade. The film
of black thinned out clings to its edge, stubborn
as a peeled-off secret come back

to claim its kiss. How you tease it,
stepped out of it the way you abandoned
that funereal suit whose tailored fit
says you belong back inside.

The corpse in the coffin: a man
who slept with you, whose lips

you cannot split apart again. His mouth
invited you in to confirm

that there is no final tongue touch
blistering within. You are no longer one.
The stitch that bound you came loose
ahead of the needle swallowing the thread.

Your lover and you
were never meant to be intact
completely, only temporarily connected
until that night you lean away, two

pieces of split wood. The black knot
from which you both take root
forces each of you to opposite ends.
Then what happens? In closing the book

of intimate glances, you learn
who leaves whom behind.
You looked at him and
the dead man rose to say goodbye,

not looking up or down
the way the preachers always say,
not looking in or out—
not even looking back.

Widower's Welcome

for my mother

Only dead wives buried near my mother's grave.
They huddle in the rainy season beneath
bouquets of wet carnations. No tears from the men

who come here—just sweat and soaked coats.
That masculine musk released into the humid air
awakens my desire. I'm too aware of living, sorry

these women exchanged the company of men
for stone, smooth and hard as their husbands' backs.
The wish to disappear into the rigid creases of the spine,

behind tense muscle, below bone, granted.
I have known such pleasure, and I will grieve its loss,
imagining my mother longs for the man who filled

her breath with his. She now sleeps without my father's
song inside her mouth, her tongue a hollow print
of her lover's tongue. And my father, partnered

again—another wife, a different song. Silence
greets him at the cemetery gate, and ushers him
to memory. I inhale his scent and try to understand

why a woman dies and in her loneliness discovers

how to stir the ghost of passion, suddenly alive

from the rigid facial tissue to the empty muscle of the foot.

Body, Anti-Body

I'm lifeless because lifeless
gifts are what my partner gives
me: words that gnash without teeth,
limp orchids masked as kisses,
the sexless fuck of neglect.

His lust became wallpaper-
tame after only a year
in his bed. His mouth forgot
how to suck and gnaw and lock
itself around those tender nubs

that please me. Displeased, my flesh
began to seek those strangers
generous with touch. With them
I'm not a name, I'm body.
I'm not a ghost, I'm living skin

that craves the skirmish scars
of passion and taking stock
in the dark of nick and bite
and bruise, the stench of triumph
thickening air. These men act

on instinct, with violence
that drives and thrusts and imposes
pure punishment upon me.

I love my sudden lovers
anonymous and loutish.

I know I'm alive when I
mend with stitches, when my heart
hammers against its lonely
cell, grunt and groan companions
in delightful exertion.

Oh, the temporary itch
of fingertip and tongue. I'm
as famished as the street
devouring all sensation
at any point two people

meet. Wink and I'll respond. Smile,
I'll exist. Detachment drops
me dead into the sinkhole
of my partner's sleep. Therein
my curse: to be the sweetheart

fierce with sweats, to taper down
to thinning bone and shrinking
marrow, to mad shriek without
throat, to palpable shadow
drilling its nose to the wall.

PART III

~ ~ ~

I am aware of your body and its dangers.
I spread my cloak for you in leafy weather
Where other fugitives and other strangers
Will put their mouths together.

Thomas James, "Reasons"

Breaking Down Picasso's Minotaur

You tell me you're tired of sex,
that with age your balls grew heavy as paperweights
for the dull pendulum of your cock.

The black hair on your chest disappears
quietly. The urge to surprise my sleep
with your tongue's heat has cooled off.

Yes, love, you are getting old,
and I'll remember fondly that taut guitar
in your voice that strummed a thousand

nights. Each song a serenade
to the miracle of my nape's arch
completing the half-circle of your throat

as we locked together in the pleasure
of my being taken from behind.
Your breath pushed into mine

and we reinvented
the direction of the moan.
Remember it. Rehearse the sounds and

erase Picasso's bulls.
You lost yourself inside the Minotaur's
uneven eyes, inside the swollen lip—

rectangular as a trough—
inside the nostrils pressed flat
on the mural of a face.

Exhausted beast.
It will hold its pose until its hide
decays right off the paper.

Death takes no canvas to its
art. How can I still sleep
with you, you ask, when you are

older than my father
and I'm young enough to be
your son? Because, old man,

only you know how to ripen
the night like a pomegranate. The brown
moon of my ass craves your hands.

Hold it firmly like you used to.
Split it open. Grant me
the warm explosion of rubies.

Welts off the Bone

We're up-ending the turrets, tipping the church like a bowl of beans, brown you and brown me, you on top of me, me on top of you. We're scattering our widow-mothers to flatten like manholes in the street. We're pushing them in. Even the Madonna moon wants a peek.

Before I kneel to kiss your cock I remove its cross and hang it back on the wall. To open your cheeks and expose the chalice of your ass is to find the pink lips of lost Catholics.

We lock our limbs to crush the saints we don't believe in. We snap shut the pretense of altar alms, the delicacy of foreskin against cotton in the sacristan's cassock. Cry Jesus of the impalers, cry Jesus of the sacred blood, cry Jesus the overseer, the observer, the voyeur.

Nun-whisper to my ear, blow the candles out, blow me, blow you, blow us through the cavities of cocksucker skulls decaying in the graveyard. Blow the welts off the bone. Blow them.

Everything that's me inside of you softens into wet bread. Everything that's you is me. No secrets, love, pure confession. The wafer of your ear is raw is sweet.

Cuando te trago, amor, me trago a mí mismo. Contra tu llave soy la bendita copa, mi jerez, mi veneno, mi jarabe de la medianoche, mi cólico, mi canto, mi agua santa, mi aceite de olivo, mi mame, mi memo, mi mima.

God, I love to fuck you in Spanish.

Papi Love

If Papi stops loving me, I'll look for a man who acts
like a man, who opens his brown heart like
a wallet in public places, who burns slowly as a
cigarette in bed, who is unafraid to intoxicate
with his ash—a brave man, thick-nostriled, scarred,
whose only unused muscle is his inhibition. Show me

a man who can't hold back from plunging his fingers
into his lover's flesh and you've shown me a man
who can lick his hands clean of my sweat and
blood. I want to stay so pure, so elemental, so
mattered—a property essential as air
that practices its warm seductions in the lung.

Give me a man who describes my every crease and mole and
knuckle, and I have a man who can cradle my entire
body in his mouth. I need that god, that judge, that
father who hugs me like the son he never wanted
to give up, who wants me back inside his womb, unborn,
undressed across the sheets that helped conceive me.

A man made me a man and only a man
can hurt me, unlocking my lips from the
copper nub of his nipple, withholding the milky
dish of his hand from my thirst. A selfish man
becomes barren and chokes on his own white dust.
A man generous as a church is going to be

my man, my give-it-to-me-till-it-doesn't-hurt
Papi, sideburns graying to an overcast sky, groin flash-
ing with lightning, hairy chin that tickles down my back
like rain. Ask me who loves me and I'll tell you
who I am: I am the keystone held intact by the arc
of his arms, I am the texture that exists at the command of

his touch, the scent of pressed carnations dead
until it comes alive beneath his nose. I am
that shadow of a man. It's because he steps into the sun
that I am. It's because he breathes that I have
breath. It's because I wake up in the morning
with the wide clock of my face still beautiful

and ticking that I know I'm worth a man.
If Papi stops loving me he can't be that man
and I'll kick the tired animals of his hands
off my path. If Papi stops loving me he never was
a man. Without me he'll never be a man because I am
what makes a man a man.

Transference

A warm bubble grows inside me; your body buoys
off my back. I twist my neck. I see right through your tongue:
its brown vessels constrict into the lines on dry mud.

Breathe into the dusty fissure of my ear and coax
me from the ground. My hands have dug into the soil
but will fracture at the wrists because they didn't do

what hands should have done when a man becomes a
scavenger and attacks. They have ceased to be hands.
What breed of flower comes to life from semen and

blood? I will hear it break the earth in my sleep.
In the meantime I forgive you. That tender question: *Why
do you cry?* I'm convinced comes from your mouth, though

you do not speak. Those words will haunt me
as I dream I till a plot of flesh, yanking veins
like weeds. When I extract a heart, turnip-stiff, shame

will overwhelm me. Only an ingrate would deny this find
its beauty. *Why do you cry?* I will ask. *You want it back,
all that I took with me to leave you barren and empty?*

Changing Your New Year's Tune

Any bon voyage excites this way: the last calendar
box, the last night
you expect to live

picking up man after strange
man, wiping clean each whiskey-hot mouth,
clumsy as the one before.

The next one, you promised,
must thirst for your sweat
without spitting it out at the hotel door.

The dance hall ceiling, cupola-domed, illuminates
with a single light, sequin, glitter, glass
lip and tinseled hat.

The band plays merengues. The floor
hosts a battalion of heels—one scuff mark
rubbing off another. The music sways an orgy

of hips. And you, bored, a puzzle in white
silk beneath a black rayon vest, sneak a finger to the crotch
to check if your zipper's up.

A drunk Spaniard sings to you in Catalán, proving
for his Middle Eastern girl in platforms that Mexicans

don't understand the dialect. The girl,

switching conversation,
ponders at the likeness of the barefoot,
penis-fondling infants of impoverished México and India.

You want to tell her that last week
in Vegas you collected wedding rings by pulling
them off your intoxicated one-night lovers

with your teeth. One desperate man forced
his fingers to your throat and made you
swallow it. You belched a metallic aftertaste.

Usually it's a storm that reminds you
of your poverty days: eight years old,
you suckled on a chipped key

in the rain—a childhood wish
to be struck by lightning, to be cartoon-
charred to a pair of startled eyes

inside a jagged blot of ink. You'd blink and sputter
like a power surge. You'd shut your eyes
and turn yourself off to the world.

The Spaniard persists spitting in Catalán.
You ask his girlfriend if she can afford
to have you fuck him into silence.

She doesn't answer, distracted by the bat dancing
with the chandelier. You join the frieze of faces.
The flickering wings pinch every drunken eye.

Trace

Draw the bone
down the middle of my back with
your breath
and tell me who
creeps behind you that cries
that half moan
you mistake for mine.
It's not me
who shudders when you press
yourself against my skin.
The hair on your chest
grows cold with
unfamiliarity.
Your foot's arch prefers
the company of your calf.
When you rise from the bed
my sweat peeling off
your body makes me wince,
makes me smell
the other side of the door.
Your fingertip slides
across my lips and remembers
nights my lips have never kissed.
I am not deceived—
the taste betrays the pleasures
of a warmer room.

Breads That Hunger

I make love to a man with a button fetish. Correction:
a man makes love to my shirt. He yanks each piece of
plastic with his teeth and swallows it, then inserts the
cusp of his tongue into the buttonhole. I slip out of the
sleeves and off the bed and he scarcely notices. Later,
he comes looking for me; my shirt slumped across his
shoulder. It looks as if I have shed my skin—the fantasy
of meeting the train on the rusty tracks comes to life.
Buttonless, I have been stripped of everything that
holds me together. He tells me he can replace the shirt.
I tell him he can keep me.

Other Fugitives and Other Strangers

The nightclub's neon light glows red with anxiety
as I wait on the turning lane. Cars blur past,
their headlights white as charcoal.
I trust each driver not to swerve. I trust each stranger
not to kill me and let me cross
the shadow of his smoky path.
Trust is all I have for patrons at the bar:
one man offers me a line, one man buys the kamikaze,
another drinks it. Yet another wraps his arm
around my waist. I trust him not to harm my body
as much as he expects his body to remain unharmed.
One man asks me to the dance floor, one asks me
to a second drink, another asks me home.
I dance, I drink, I follow.
I can trust a man without clothes.
Naked he conceals no weapons, no threat
but the blood in his erection. His bed unfamiliar,
only temporarily. Pillows without loyalty
absorb the weight of any man, betray
the scent of the men who came before.
I trust a stranger's tongue to tell me
nothing valuable. It makes no promises
of truth or lies, it doesn't swear commitments.
The stranger's hands take their time exploring.
Undisguised, they do not turn to claws or pretend
artistic skill to draw configurations on my flesh. They
are only human hands with fingertips

unsentimental with discoveries, without nostalgia
for what they leave behind. I trust this stranger
not to stay inside me once he enters me.
I trust him to release me from the blame
of pleasure. The pain I exit with no greater
than the loneliness that takes me to the bar.
He says good night, I give him back
those words, taking nothing with me that is his.
The front door shuts behind me, the gravel
driveway ushers me away. The rearview mirror
loses sight of threshold, house, sidewalk, street.
Driving by the nightclub I pass a car
impatient on the turning lane. My hands are cold
and itch to swerve the wheel, to brand
his fender with the fury of my headlights.
But I let this stranger live
to struggle through the heat and sweat
of false affections, anonymous and
borrowed like the glass that washed my prints
to hold another patron's drink.

The Blue Boy Next Door
(And His Lover)

after Zephyrus, *a painting by Tino Rodríguez*

For the wayward angel any bird's wings will do—
the pheasant's, certainly, because it flowers in the hunt.
Or perhaps its distant cousin's, the peacock, coquettish
in its courtship frock. In any case your body craves

attention. Your fingers are aflame from tearing the teal
sheets on those nights your lover leaves you. You cry
into the whiteness of your hands until they're pink enough
to make the bedroom glow and wake the neighbors up.

If you press your palm prints to the window's glass
will the neighbors pity the pair of starlings smoldering
across the street? If you bind the creatures by the necks
will they cease their shrieking? Drama queen, every

blue inch of you screams for a wound. It's the only way
to secure your man's return. When he comes he's yellow
with famine and will need to sink his teeth into your flesh.
He has already eaten out your heart and can never kill you

that way again. But you want him nonetheless; no other
mouth knows the fierce pulse of your blood. And none
can match your stare, so heavy you bruise when you blink.
And what do the neighbors think when you toss a kiss

and it strikes the wall like rock? Let them listen in.
Your lover's at the door, the show will soon begin. Once more
you play the injured prey and he the eager predator
whose hunger quickens with the smell of easy game.

Latin Lover

Let me shave you like a porn star.
You spread open the suggestion wide
as your chest, your hairy nipples a pair of
crop circles on the white torso.
My clothes are a pile of wrinkles at my feet.

I'm smooth and brown
as the sand that escapes the fingers to drown
into the sea. You are a patchwork of black—
armpits, spidery navel, a burst of pubic hair
prickly as a pincushion. *Turn around,*

you command, suddenly a director.
I crave the cheesecake I refused
at dinner, which your boyfriend devoured
when you left the table, your room number
sticky on my wrist like the blueberry syrup.

He monopolized the breadbasket.
I knew that second helping of dessert
was going to be his greatest pleasure
tonight. I straddle your groin, bend down
to kiss you. Your mouth reminds me of

your boyfriend's mouth—cheesecake, chardonnay,
the dry aftertaste of insincere flattery.
He said you had to have uncircumcised Latino

every now and then. Your weakness—that
and Russian nesting dolls. Your pale fingers

slide down my ass. You ask if I fear
getting cut as the sharp razor slithers up
my scrotum, down my inner thigh. I shake my head.
I've hosted more dangerous guests.
I know the risk and love for things exotic.

The Strangers Who Find Me in the Woods

after Thomas James

The strangers in the woods must mimic squirrels and crackle
with the undergrowth. They must not flinch at the cruelty
of breaking golden leaves with their feet, or of interring stones.
And like any of these deciduous trees in autumn they must be

stingy with shadow and move deceptively across the sludge.
I listen to these strangers stirring with the evenings. I invent paths
for them to the soft edge of the lake. Each descent is as graceful
as a sinking ship, but less tragic somehow because these strangers

don't possess a lung. I cannot hear them breathe, yet the air
is all whispers, all sighs—the same ethereal muscle that rubs
the color off the foliage. I lost my way out of the woods on the night
every bird went south or numb. A plump rat snatched the moon

and dragged it by the white rope of its tail. The strangers were
a cloak of silhouettes flattening against a trunk like bark.
I must have disappeared among them because the mouth I touched
was not my own and was cruelly closing in on someone's rib. I carried

such a bite on me, an arc of green and yellow on my side from the man
who said he loved me. In that darkness I knew as much about him
as I did of the amputee swimming his way up the hill with his
only arm. So this is the home of the unturned stone where

the fugitive keeps his kiss! Archeologists will discover a paradise
in the place no touch died of neglect. Is it any wonder all things
forgotten or abandoned find their way here? The winter is back, so too
the bloated body of a book I tossed over the bridge last week.

And there on the bench, is my old smoking habit, a cigarette
glowing on my mouth like a beacon. I'm patient, waiting for the fugitive
to claim me as his own. I'm as wise as any stranger here, alone but with
the knowledge that the grief of separation is always brief.

Danza Macabre

Your wreath declares: *I celebrate my coffin because it keeps me*
longer than my mother. Wood polished to patience as the tantrum
of your body wastes no time to soften. As your grudges forgive
themselves, as your indiscretions uproot from their hiding places
to crawl away like larvae, as the stones of your gossip tumble off

your tongue, you're gratified somehow that all your flaws
and all your crimes will be absolved. That's what you believed
into the final hour, and found comfort in this fantasy while I
nailed my doubts to my skull and said nothing. Now the soil tightens
its grip on your coffin and my thoughts take wing: if what you said

were true, lover, cemeteries would be the cheeriest homes
with its laughter six feet deep and a nursery of cherubs
blowing at the pinwheels on the Catholic stones. And somewhere
behind the water tank would wait the caretaker in his cardinal
frock ready to pounce with confetti. What a treat to frolic

with the dead as their souls climb like carnival balloons,
music from the organ grinder driving the monkey to madness.
How fortunate the deceased like you, stiff-fingered, lock-jawed,
unburdening your bodies without effort, the seven sinful sisters
settling to clear the murky water of your blood. Even the fiery

mood of your eyes cools off like lava, and you appear human
again. Perhaps even humane. Death is so tolerant and forgiving

even with those who were not. You can take your make-believe
afterlife with you. I am alive, and the breathing can allow for other
theories. In my cosmos of karma, the dead swim like fetuses

in their personal purgatories and must drown their way out
of their earthly deeds. The scratch and bruise come back
to roost in the hand that fathered them. The bark and scream return,
clotting the throat until it implodes. Even the prodigal kick leaps
up to the bone, demanding to be sheltered again in the quick-tempered

spring of the knee. Past offenses multiply the memory cells of the flesh,
bubbling the brain into oblivion. That is how I see you now: fury coma
self-consumed into spasms. Wouldn't it be nice for the victimized?
I suppose however that neither you nor I will be humored, that the end
has surprised you as much as it will me when the sky closes up

like the fist we've both seen as often as night. At long last, when my body
also dims to gray, we'll be equals, companion corpses, gracefully
retired like a pair of ballet slippers, predator indistinguishable from
prey. Let the rosaries murmur that lovers make peace in their graves.
Let the sun search for spectral kisses. Let the moon bless the padlock

as the living leave and shut the gate. No fugitives permitted here—only
debts and those who resolve them. Goodbye, my former love, be
patient as my body marvels at the world without you. In a year or decade
I'll be dead and we'll converse again through all eternity. Partnered in
our favorite dance, your phantom holler with my ghostly screech.